LABELED

The things you don't want to see…

BY: LATARCHA JACKSON

Labeled

Printed in the United States of America

First Edition, 2020

ISBN   978-0-578-71978-8

AuthorLaTarchaJackson@gmail.com

Acknowledgements

I would like to first thank God for his mercy and his grace. Through my trials and tribulations, it was God who kept me, and I will not take it for granted. I am blessed and highly favored. Thank you to my parents. My mom Patricia (Sunshine) no matter what I said I wanted to do she would tell me to go for it even if I didn't know how I was going to do it. She would be there every step of the way. She taught me to trust God. To do what I can, and God would do what I can't. My dad Will (Action Jackson) he taught me the hustle to be a go getter and to always have your own, be your own boss and get to the money and to never lend money that you can't afford not to get back. With both of my parents instilled in me when people meet me the walk away saying Red is HELL!!

My two beautiful daughters Shandricka & Le'Asha (My heartbeats) my reasons I strive to be the best that I can be. Being your mother is two of the best gifts God could ever blessed me with. Thank you for giving me your ideas and your input on my book. Thank you for understanding I'm not perfect but I have always tried to be the best mom I could possibly be. You both have turned out to be two intelligent, independent, respectful young ladies. I love you so much. Promise (R.I.P 2020), Kookie, Oreo, Twixx, Leonardo thanks for being the most awesome pets ever.

@Royal- T Empire www.allthingsroyalt.com thank you for my beautiful book cover & apparel. I gave you my vision and you brought it to life. I pray that your business will continue to prosper.

To my siblings Lisa, Will Jr, Johnny thank you for accepting that I am mom favorite (joking) each one of you bring something different to my life and what you bring is what I need thank you & I love you for that. Demetrius (stepbrother), Belinda (stepmom) & Alison thank you for being a great addition to my life. I appreciate your support

To my cousin Pam thank you for taking the time to take me step by step on how to become an author and I know I may have worked your nerves. But you never showed it thank you for being patient with me and sending me encouraging words.

To my sister from another mother and business partner LaChunda I have laughed, cried, vent, ask for all type of advice. You are that person when you say let you know if I need you, I know you mean it good or bad because you will be there. I thank you for that and I know it's only a matter of time our business will flourish. (Seize the Day Event Planning & Party Rentals)

Xavier thank you for being you because it helped me evolve in the woman I am today. I will always love you for that. No regrets just lessons & blessings. Xavier Jr thank you for being the son I never birthed it was a joy to watch you grow into manhood, I love you and my bonus kids.

To my circle of TRUE friends that turn into family my list is small, but I love each one of you, I appreciate you, thank you for the prayers and support.

My family is huge, but I love each one of you thank you for the thoughts, prayers and support.

Chapter 1

Stepping out on my patio on this beautiful morning looking up at the beautiful blue sky I feel the breeze brush against my skin. Oh, what a day oh what a day! The birds are chirping, and the weather is great. It was dreadful that I could not be outside long I had to go back on the inside to prepare for my day. I looked over at the clock it was 9:24 am it was a shock to me because normally on Saturday's I am up by 7 am to start my day to cook breakfast for the kids and clean up the apartment. One of the reasons I love to get up early is to enjoy peaceful alone time. Once my kids wake up it will no longer be quiet in the apartment. I rarely receive a good morning from the kids I get mommy I am hungry. I often dream of living in a nice home, owning my own business, being married, financial stable, nice car, kids, the ability to help others, however, my reality is I live in an apartment that goes by your income, I am a single mother with two kids, a customer service rep living check to check & my car barely gets me from A to B, and can't help others because I can barely help myself... It may not be the best life but it's my life & I'm blessed & thank God for it. I do not have a man in my life. My grandma once said it's better to have half of a man than no man at all I wonder what she was telling me is to have two men to make one good man. Well, that remains to be seen because I don't want half of a man.

As I was washing dishes breaking news was on tv and Amber alert was issued for a 12-year-old black girl abducted from her bedroom. Her mother stated she went into her daughter's room to wake her up to get ready for her game at Jackson Park she is a cheerleader, and she was not in her bed. A picture of her flashed on the tv screen a beautiful little girl with sandy brown hair, mole on her chin & dimples she was last seen wearing hello kitty pajamas, and her hair was braided in cornrows.

Her mom was begging, crying & pleading for help to find her daughter, and asking the kidnappers to please bring her back. She is a diabetic and needs her insulin. The mother & daughter live in the same apartment complex that I live in. It is scary because it could have been one of my kids we are also on the bottom floor of my apartment. I'm praying that the little girl will be found safely and back home where she belongs. I have a daughter around the same age who is a diabetic as well and I know how stressful that could be while your child is with you it's even more stressful and hurtful when your child is not around. As a parent, you want to make sure the child is being cared for properly.

I am making sure the kids get dressed to go with me to run errands it takes forever we only have one bathroom and my 13 years old LaTrice forgets because she is always in there the longest.

My 2-year-old Serenity is going through her terrible two-stage, and she gets a little out of hand with her tantrums she gets several butt whooping's. You would think she would realize that I am the mom that will not tolerate the tantrums. I can't wait until she is 3 and hopefully it will get better. Let's just say I am in desperate need of a vacation to relax and get away from my day-to-day life if only for a weekend. I can come back to reality with a clear head not feeling so overwhelmed. Finally, all dressed and ready to run errands in between errands I will try to include a little fun for my girls. I learned as a teenager always leave the house looking and smelling good because that one time that you don't you will see someone you know and their first thought, she must be doing bad. I will not be caught slipping! Unless when I walk to the mailbox, I normally look any kind of way 1995 Freak-Nik t-shirt satin cap on my head oversize jogging pants whatever the first thing I see to throw on.

I know it is 2016 but I couldn't let my 1995 Freak-Nik shirt go 1994 & 1995 was the best Freak-Nik ever. Hitting the streets with all the traffic hitting the clubs with DJ Kizzy Rock on the 1's and 2's. Back in the day, I was fine as wine Coca-Cola shape body but now let's just say I am a two-liter bottle. I can blame 30% of my weight on having kids and 70% on bad relationships and stress it causes me to overeat and eat all the wrong things. Even when the relationship is going well the first thing, they want to do is feed you. I have not been in a relationship in a long time. In my last relationship, he was a drug dealer, abusive, mentally & physically. I was not attracted to him. He felt the money he was making & giving me would cover up the fact of how unhappy I was, and he could treat me any kind of way. I also looked over the fact I had no connection with him. Even though I saw his original labels I thought he would change. I had to realize my worth and to know that I deserve better.

I was nothing that I was doing to make him treat me the way that he did, but he had internal demons and he felt I was never going anywhere. I took a lot of abuse & felt like nothing I said or did was good enough for him. The money had me blinded and in my head, I felt I needed it. I prayed myself out of the situation it took some time, but it worked. My oldest daughter LaTrice's father Richard was killed I have not been able to find anyone close to loving me the way he did and me loving him we were high school sweethearts. He was the love of my life, but he was killed by mistaken identity.

Even though Richard was a big-time drug dealer he invested. He always did community service, and he was very humble. He knew how to be low-key with his transactions and never crossed anyone with a bad deal. He treated me like a queen, I know it was wrong for him to sell drugs and maybe that was his dark side but what I saw in him was not a drug dealer. I saw a kindhearted, loving man.

He had an identical twin brother Reginald he lived more of a dangerous life. He has robbed people, broken in houses, made bad drug deals & carjacked people at gunpoint. He had plenty of enemies. Due to the fact they shared the same face being identical twins. The love of my life was killed by a lowlife drug dealer looking for his brother. The guy did not ask any questions just started shooting and shot Richard 4 times. His twin Reginald is serving life in prison for killing the guy that killed Richard, he saw it all happen while he was walking out the gas station and he unloaded his pistol on the guy. He has now turned his life around in prison and reads the bible and wants to be a jailhouse preacher.

I feel it's too late for all of that I have lost the love of my life and there is nothing I can do, or he can do to bring him back. My baby girl Serenity's father Seneca he was extremely sexy we met at a Walmart and couldn't keep our eyes off each other.

I went through the self-checkout, and he followed me to the car. I heard someone say pretty lady can I talk to you for a minute? he asked. We talked for almost 30 minutes in the parking lot then we eventually exchanged numbers the chemistry we had was powerful just in that short conversation. We would talk daily we would hang out I was liking him and the way he treated me it seems he was liking me too. Could he be the one to fill this void of me losing Richard? I would never forget he called me on a Thursday and told me to pack myself a weekend bag and don't forget a swimsuit. He also said he would pay for the babysitter for LaTrice how I could say no to this. Seneca told me to be ready tomorrow by 5 pm. I immediately got off the phone and called my nana to see if she would babysit, she said yes.

I got off work and went to the store to find myself a nice swimsuit and something cute to wear to bed because my bed wear is a big t-shirt or an old nightgown with holes in it which is nothing sexy about that.

Finally, it's Friday I could not sleep last night because I was so excited. Thinking where he is taking me. At work, I was counting down the time to 3 pm to go straight home to shower get dressed and wait for him to pick me up. My nana already was picking up LaTrice from school & I packed her clothes & nana stopped by to pick them up. All I had to do was call to hear my baby voice. We have never had sex before, but I am pretty sure if we are spending the weekend together, I am sure to spread my legs for him. Everything was moving so fast, but I loved every moment of it. I wonder is this the man I prayed for is this the man I ask God to design just for me?

Chapter 2

It's 5:02 pm I heard a knock at the door. I didn't want to be too anxious I waited for the next knock to open the door. Who is it I asked? He said it's Seneca baby open the door. When I opened the door, he had the most beautiful roses. He handed them to me and kissed me on my cheek it gave me butterflies in my stomach. I placed the roses in a vase and placed water in them. Baby are you ready he asked? I said yes, my bag is on the sofa. He grabbed my bags and closed my blinds and said I will be in the car make sure you lock up. As I walk through my small apartment making sure the other blinds are closed and everything is cut off, I am smiling like a child on Christmas with a tree full of gifts. Everything is locked up and I am ready to go.

As I go outside, he is waiting on the passenger side to open the door for me. I got and he closed the door and I notice a nice scent in his car, and he was playing slow jams. It felt so peaceful as we were listening to music and singing along. Neither one of us could sing and that was what made it more fun and meaningful because we were being ourselves. Still unsure where we are going but I am enjoying the ride. I don't want to ask him because it may ruin the moment. We rode for 3 hours, and he stopped by a nice restaurant for us to eat at called LaChunda's steak house. The food was delicious and after we left, we proceeded to go to our destination. After I eat, I get sleepy all I remember is singing a song by Gerald Levert and I woke up and saw beautiful water around me. Seneca says baby we are here. Singing, laughing, joking, and sleeping as we were riding, I didn't pay attention we are at Bailey's Beach I had the biggest smile on my face looking at the water and how beautiful it was.

Seneca had already preplanned us a suite as I walked into the room it was roses in vases and rose petals on the bed and floor, candles were lit around the room, and as we stepped out on the balcony you saw sand & water it was lingerie laying on the bed and it was my size. Seneca said our first-time making love he wanted it to be special and meaningful. I must admit I was feeling special. He went to the mini-fridge and pulled out fruit and wine. He went to the bathroom, and I heard the water running unsure what was taking so long. He came out and said my water was waiting on me. I walk in it was a big jacuzzi tub with bubbles, a glass of wine on the side, strawberries, and grapes in a bowl. I immediately got in and enjoyed the warm jacuzzi he joined me at first, we were just talking about life and how relaxing it is from our day-to-day life. Then we begin to kiss passionately as his hands start to rub on my clit and my hands start to rub on his nice size penis.

He whispered in my ear and said I want you to lay in the bed and spread your legs. I didn't hesitate to get out of the jacuzzi to dry off to lay on the bed he told me no need to dry off because his goal is to keep me wet. I laid on the bed he spread my legs wider than I already had it and he started to lick, suck on my vagina. As he took his tongue in, out, up, and down, I got wetter and wetter than I felt something go in my anal it was his finger. He started to finger fuck my asshole while he was finger fucking my ass while he was sucking on my pussy. I never had that done to me before and it was driving me insane, and I let out a loud scream and said I AM ABOUT TO CUM! He sucked all the cum out of me and slid his dick in and started stroking and going deeper and deeper. Everything was feeling so good, and the mood felt so right neither one of us thought about a condom. Him going in and out inside of me I was getting so weak coming back too back and the way he would look at me with a smirk on his face and kiss me I couldn't take any more he said baby cum with me next thing I knew it felt like an explosion inside of me we both was moaning & groaning and bodily fluids collided with each other. It was a magical moment it felt so good. After we were done, we showered together. Time for the beach!

We look nice in our swimwear walking the beach holding hands watching the waves in the ocean feeling the sand on our feet. We laid a blanket down and watch the sunset sipping on a strawberry daiquiri.

It was so romantic after the sunset fireworks were shooting up in the sky, I love fireworks. We headed back to the hotel for another round however I wanted to return the favor I told him to get naked and lay on the bed. I begin to kiss his neck then slowly kiss him until I got to his dick. I started to suck his dick and the more I sucked the harder it grew the noises he was making were turning me on and I started to get wet. I wrapped a fruit roll-up around his dick which made me suck it vigorously.

I was curious would I finish the candy before he came in my mouth. I decided to switch it up on him & crawled and got on top of his dick and started to ride him I looked down at him and gave him a smirk because I knew I was riding the hell out of his dick. Then as the ride started to get intense, I started to feel his dick throb in me, he grabbed my hips and started throwing his dick back. I felt myself about to cum and I said oh shit I am about to cum he said I am to I tried to get up before he came inside of me, he grabs me closer and said no baby I want you to feel all of this inside of you he was holding me so tight then he yelled out oh shit its coming baby I loudly I screamed me too.

When we were done, I lay on his chest. We ended up falling asleep in each other arms when we woke up, we looked over to the patio and the sun was rising. We got up showered to enjoy our day by eating, shopping, we also went to Ripley's believe it or not and the Hollywood wax museum, we took plenty of pics.

We both agreed that we wanted to go back to our suite to watch the sunset. We made it in time for us to get there freshen up and change into something comfortable. As we watched the sunset, he looked at me and told me he loved me I was so, wrapped up in the moment I told him I love him too. As we lay in the bed, he started telling me the reason why he loves me and how he doesn't ever want to be without me it was like music to my ears.

Chapter 3

Nine months later and we are still going strong, and we welcomed our baby girl Serenity. That's how

Serenity came about. My whirlwind love. Seneca moved in with me when I was 5 months pregnant because I was high risk, and he stated his lease was up in his apartment. I know it may sound dumb, but I have never been to where he lived before. I have been to his job but never where he laid his head. We talked, texted and on the weekend, he would sometimes spend the night I never thought of visiting him. Even though I live in an apartment that goes by my income I knew our plan was not to live there long and for us to get a house together. He asked me for one of my bills to do and address change at his job and to let his family know where he lives now. I didn't think anything of it because I wanted him to feel comfortable living with me to feel like we are working toward something.

Sunday morning, we are getting the kids up for church they say a family prays together stays together and that is what I am trying to do. I like to sit in the middle and around the fourth row. I am so focused on the word most times I feel like the pastor be talking directly to me. Pastor Haynes preached a great sermon he preached on forgiveness and letting the past go. I looked over to Seneca and I noticed it was tears rolling down his eyes. I passed him a tissue and grabbed his hand as comfort. When we walked out of the church a lady came up to me and said how can you be with him, I said excuse me? And she walked away. I asked Seneca who it was he said he didn't know. Even though I didn't bring it back up to him it bothered me all that night on why a total stranger would come up to me and make that statement. All I know is Seneca had been so great with LaTrice as well as with our daughter together Serenity and he treats me like a queen, even though my bills are not much he pays all of them and he works daily & comes home to us every night I couldn't ask for a better man.

Seneca received a call from his mom and said on Saturday they would be having a cookout for his dad's 60th birthday and to make sure he come and to bring us. I was excited to meet his other family members and to wonder if they are as crazy as my family. I went to the mall that week and got us a new outfit and shoes. For some reason, it seems as if he didn't want to go and be around his other family and I asked him why not he just stated some of them get on his nerves. I understood that because some of my family members get on my nerves. He told me we will probably get there on time and not stay there all night I was cool with it because I know Serenity gets fidgety at times. I was looking forward to it because we never are around other people it's mostly always us and the last time, we've been out of town is when I conceived Serenity.Saturday finally came. I got up cleaned up the house and cooked breakfast for everyone and showered.

I like to lay down and relax after I eat & clean before I leave the house. Seneca was in a flirtatious mood I was bending down in the closet to get the shoes I just purchased, and I couldn't even stand up good he slid his dick in and started having sex with me from the back. When the kids are home, we have silent sex even though it is so hard for me to do because his dick is so good, and he hit every corner of my pussy and he goes deep. I want to lay in the bed all day now because he has me tired. He knows how to make me feel good. I know I can't because I am looking forward to meeting his family. Kids dressed; Seneca dressed, & I am dressed finally we can get ready to go to his parents' house it is a 30-minute drive. Normally when we ride together, we laugh, talk and sing he was very quiet as if he had a lot on his mind. Hey babe, he said what's up cupcake (the nickname he gave me) are you ok we have never had a quiet ride like this. He said he was fine just dread having to see some of his family members.

I perked him up a little one of our songs came on the radio and I needed a background singer, so he begins to sing together while the kids were in the back seat looking at us. We heard a ding in the car. It was the gaslight he pulled into the gas station to get gas and snacks. As he was pumping the gas, I heard a guy say Black is that you? Seneca said oh what's up Slick how have you been? Slick said he was good then I heard him say Black when did you get out? In my head, I said out! Out of where? Seneca told him he had been out about 3 ½ years now. I never knew he had been locked up and when we had conversations during the get to know each other process, he did not mention that at all. When he got in the car, I did not want to mention it because we had the kids, and we were on the way to meet the family. I was quiet the rest of the ride and he would look over to me from time to time, but I had my shades on and he didn't think I noticed it. It seems like the 30-minute ride was a four-hour drive because of how quiet it was I even stopped eating my snacks and I love my snacks.

Chapter 4

Pulling up at his parents' house he opened the back door to get Serenity out of the car seat walked around and opened the door for LaTrice and me. He had cousins sitting outside smoking and drinking. We walked on the inside and saw the older crew and his parents he introduced us to everyone that didn't already know us. A lot of his family members did not know that he recently had a baby girl because he does not socialize with them. He found two empty seats and brought them to LaTrice and me. He was still holding Serenity passing her around because people wanted to hold her & play with her. I heard someone come out of the restroom it was a female she said oh hell no I thought I would be gone before you got here, and she stated she refuse to be in the same room with him & she stormed outside.

Everyone in the room brushed it off however for me that is something else that I need to discuss once we get home. Even though the food and the company were good now I'm more ready to go home because it is obvious its things we need to discuss.We finally made it home exhausted I got the girls ready for bed he showered, and I showered last. By the time I got out of the shower, he was asleep. I tried to wake him I told him I needed to talk to him about some things. He said cupcake can we talk about it in the morning because he had been drinking and he is extremely tired. I agreed. When I have this conversation, I need him to be sober. All night I once again tossed and turned to wonder what can be going on and why he has not been totally honest with me. All type of things has been crossing my mind to me he is a great guy but who was he before and is he still that same guy just in disguise?

Morning is finally here now I can get my answers, I get up to cook breakfast for the family and he was going to work to do overtime he normally does not work on a Sunday. I wanted to set the mood and give him breakfast in bed to ease the conversation in, but it did not work he grabbed a paper plate put his food on it and said he was running late for work he kissed me and said he will call me on his break. All I could say was ok. Being in love with him is beginning to be a mystery because my mind is so uneasy. As far as for my girls and me it is time to prepare for church. I decided for us to all dress in the same color and probably go out to eat and visit my mom afterward. Going into the church I take Serenity to the Nursery and take LaTrice to the children's church. I love to be able to praise the Lord in peace. Pastor Haynes spoke on taking the mask off and revealing who you are and not allowing the devil to take over your life and be a victim to your past. Walking out of the church I noticed that same lady from last Sunday walking over to me.

She said I see he is not with you today you must know the truth, or you knew and didn't care. I asked her for the truth about what can she share with me that she may think you know about him. She started laughing she said your sleeping with a monster, and you don't know, and you have him around your kids. What is your name? I asked her she said, Lisa. Hello Lisa, my name is Denise, and it seems to me that you have some things you need to tell me please share! I am not about to get into it on church grounds you need to do your research and beware she stated, and she walked away. Nice I could be I said Lisa what you're not about to continue to do is walk up to me with these subliminal messages after church services. Either you going to tell me what you are trying to insinuate or say nothing to me at all. After this eventful conversation, I did not have the energy to go see nana I was ready to go home and wait on Seneca to get home. Stopped grabbed dinner did not feel like cooking, got home, kids bathe, and were in bed. While in the shower I hear Seneca come in the door.

I didn't want to bombard him with questions as soon as got home when I got out of the shower, I greeted him, fixed his plate, and allow him to shower to wind down. I was determined I will get the answers I need tonight! While he was in the shower, I get a knock on the door it was a sheriff they asked no a Seneca Patterson lives at this address and I said no because I was afraid it may mess up my section 8 if they knew someone else was here other than my kids and I. I didn't want to ask what it was about I didn't want to look guilty, the man said OK & left. When Seneca got out of the shower, I told him that a sheriff came to the door looking for him. He started laughing because he thought I was playing. I told him I was serious he said that it could have possibly been his job because he changed the address and there is an off-duty sheriff doing security at his job and could be dropping off his new badge. It sounded very odd to I jumped the subject and said what is going on with that female at church and what she has on you as well as your family member that was at your parents' house?

Chapter 5

Who is that beating on the door like that at 3 am? Seneca wakes up to go to the door I'm scared. He said

"I thought you did not want anyone knowing that I was here its 3 am someone is beating on the door at this point I don't care. He went and looked out of the peephole as soon as he tried to walk away from the door the cops busted in. He said Seneca Patterson you are under arrest. I said for what officer? The officer said are there any kids here I said yes officer my two daughters he called someone to come in to go in the room with them they handcuffed me I said what did I do officer. He stated it is the procedure until we sort everything out. They took us outside and placed us on the cold concrete stoop. I had on bedroom shoes and pink short set pajamas, he had on tank top & navy-blue boxers outside in public. I was so embarrassed by neighbors looking out their window some of them walked outside to have a closer look.

I asked Seneca what did you do why are we handcuffed? The officer told us to shut up stop talking to each other before he takes me to jail with Seneca. I started to cry I overheard the officer on his walkie-talkie and said we have Seneca Patterson in handcuffs, and he will be extradited to Louisiana. At this point, I am baffled at total disbelief. The officer walked back over and told Seneca we have officers on the way to take you to the county jail until the Louisiana police department send someone to pick you up. He asked Seneca do this lady knows your charges he said no sir she is innocent she doesn't know anything. He told me to stand up and he took me off handcuff he said to go over there to talk to officer Craig to obtain more information. Seneca yelled out I'm sorry Denise I'm so sorry I love you. I had to zone him out I'm pissed and nervous not knowing what is going on. Hello, officer Craig, my name is Denise Maddox can I please check on my kids to make sure they are ok, and can you please tell me what is going on and why is he being arrested?

She walked me in to peep on the kids they were still asleep how with all the noise don't know however officer Craig stated that Seneca is being arrested and extradited to Louisiana. We have been looking for Mr. Patterson for 3 years he has not registered with the state. Registered? Yes, ma'am, he is a sex offender for the past 3 yrs he has bounced from job to job and address to address and anytime we get close he moves and switches jobs. Sex offender? He has been arrested for molesting two girls ages 11 and 15 he served 6 years and is wanted accusations of having relations with a 16 yrs. old girl and a 15 yrs. old boy. He has not been charged for the accusations because we have not been able to locate him however, we do have the DNA that can convict him of the charges now that we have him. Officer Craig may I ask how you were able to find him. We received an anonymous tip that they knew where he was because they followed you home. Due to the fact, he has not registered in 3 years, and he has two other charges pending against him he will not be

getting out anytime soon. Talk with your kids to make sure he did not touch them inappropriately.

I went over to Seneca and slapped him as hard as I could tears started rolling down his eyes. I did not care I screamed our whole relationship was a lie you had me believe that you were honest about everything and wouldn't hide anything from me. You're a monster!! How could you? Don't ever call, write or contact us in any kind of way. The police placed him in the police car & the other polices got in their car and they all drove off. I went into the house and cried until I fell asleep. I couldn't believe this was happening I'm hoping when I wake up it was all a bad dream.The sunrise came and I am still in this nightmare accepting the fact that in the early morning's everything was true is so surreal to me. I had to face my kids & act like everything is ok. I cooked them breakfast as usual turned on the tv to watch cartoons. As I was feeding Serenity, I hear her say da. Tears started to roll down my face. Being back at square one with a broken heart, making bad decisions, handling all the bills alone, I can go on and on.

I called my mom and asked could she watch the kids for a couple of hours & she said yes, I need a mental break is all I could think about. Prepared the kids to go to my nana's house to drop them off. Made it back home packed his clothes and placed them in his car. I never thought to ask why his car was in his mom name. I just assumed he had bad credit. Now it makes sense of the red flags I started to see in him. I was blindly in love I wanted to only see the good in him. I called my cousin Carmen to follow me to drop off his car with his clothes in it at his parent's house and for me to tell them everything that went on the night before. I didn't want to go into details with Carmen because sometimes she runs her mouth too much and the whole family would know, and I am not ready to talk about it any time soon with my judgmental family. Carmen stayed in the car while I went in inside to talk to them. As I was explaining to Seneca's parents what had happened, they did not seem surprised at all.

This is hurtful because if they knew the truth about everything why did they feel it was ok not to turn him in or for him to turn himself in. They accepted me, smiled in my face, feed me but did not tell me anything that was going on. That alone made me sick of my stomach. I had to get out of there. As I was walking out the door the same family member that came out the bathroom and stormed out of the house at his dad cookout was pulling up. She immediately jumped out of the car, and she screamed that bastard is not in there is he? I said what bastard? She said you know who the hell I am talking about Seneca! I said no he is in jail she said great that is where he belongs. I said my name is Denise and you are? She said her name is Genene ok Genene nice to meet you may I ask who Seneca to you is. She stated he isn't shit to me but by blood, he is supposed to be my uncle! Suppose to be? Genene stated that Seneca molested her from age 7 to 11 yrs. old and she told her mom and she said that she was having nightmares and would say anything to keep from getting in trouble for urinating in the bed almost every night.

I had tears rolling down my eyes I was devasted and hurt. I asked her did she tell her grandparents she said yes, and they said they would handle it but never did. I hugged her and told her I was so sorry that happened to her and we both cried in each other arms. Of course, nosey Carmen heard it all. And she had all types of questions when I got into her car as she is driving me home. I filled her in on everything. At this point, I care less about any backlash I am just glad that he is behind bars because he had hurt so many minors and I can begin to heal and remember not to wear a blindfold when I am falling for another man. Once our daughter gets older, I will sit her down to tell her about her father. The good, bad, ugly, & worst.

Chapter 6

A year has passed working at the same job still living in the same apartment and heart afraid to love again. After about three months Seneca has stopped trying to call or send letters. Back at being a content single parent which I am ok with it. I am far ready for being in a relationship again. I rather listen to my friends talk about their relationships. Going out to clubs and bars has never been my thing but I do know I need to go out and have some adult time. The weather is beautiful and since my breakup, I have lost a few pounds and I think I am looking good. Calling my best friend Nicole and she is not answering she must be busy doing hair. One thing about Nicole she will call me back. I never had to wait so long I called the hair salon they said she have not been in for two days. I am worried about one thing about Nicole she does not miss the money.

Her parents are deceased, and she moved down here alone we have been best friends for over ten years we normally talk daily. We are neighbors

Knocking on Nicole's door and I hear her and someone fussing I cannot make out the voice. I knocked on the door harder so they could hear me knock. Finally, Nicole came to the door, and she was crying, and I looked at her and her face was red, and she had a black eye. I screamed what happen I went into my purse to get my pistol she told me NO! put it up I am ok. Then suddenly, Tyrone come out and almost knocked me over trying to get in his car. She told me to come in she hugged me and started crying. I asked her what was wrong she said that she was tired of being with Tyrone and him hitting on her. I asked her how long he have been hitting her she said it started 3 months ago but blames her for the reason why he hits her. She says at times he comes in mad and starts arguments and has sex with her aggressively.

Last night she explained how he came in while she was in the shower he came in and grabbed her by her neck threw her on the bed and start to choke her. He put his dick in and fucked her extremely hard and almost choked her to the point she could not breathe, and her pussy started to bleed, and he pulled his dick out and stuck it in her mouth and made her swallow his cum until she started gagging. She wants out of the relationship, and she will be talking to him about ending their relationship. I called to check on Nicole she said he didn't come home for two days and walked in as if everything was ok. However, she said once she told him it was over, and she can't no longer be in a relationship with mental & physical abuse. I asked her what his response was she said he told her if he can't have you can't anybody have you. She told him he had to leave her apartment he said no he is not. As she started to cry and told him she just wants to be happy, and he does not make her happy. He goes to the bathroom & slammed the door. She said that she looked in the bedroom mirror and had to finally realize that she had to be done with him and move on. She was losing herself trying to stay with him and no longer knowing her worth. Nicole packed his clothes and placed them by the front door. She yelled in the bathroom please be gone by the time I get back home. She covered up her bruises with foundation and went back to work. Hey Denise, I turned around it was Abdul, I have not seen him in forever since high school. Hi Abdul, it's so nice to see you how have you been? He updated me on his life that he was married, and his wife passed away of cancer last year. So sorry to hear that I said with deep condolences. He asked me to update him on my life I told him I rather exchange numbers because I am in a rush to go pick up my kids before it gets too late but if you're up to it call me tonight, we can catch up he had a big smile on his face and said great. We hugged each other and we parted ways. Nicole gave me a call to let me know that she had made it to work and told Tyrone to be gone by the time she gets off.

I was relieved that she was able to get out of her abusive relationship with no issues. However, it seems as if it was too easy. I had to update her that I ran across an old school mate Abdul and that it was good to see him, and he called me that night and talked for almost four hours on the phone. It was a breath of fresh air to be able to talk about any and everything with someone with no strings attached. When my phone clicked in while talking to Nicole, I told her I would call her back because it was Abdul clicking in on the other line & I reminded her of LaTrice's hair appointment on Saturday morning. Of course, she told me I better be on time because I am always running late. Abdul asks would I like to take a walk-through Aziz Park with him and have a picnic I said yes that was just what I needed. I made it clear that I do not want anything serious just to have a friend to talk to every now & then. I was determined to be on time to have LaTrice at her hair appointment on time.

I told Abdul that we cannot have our several hours conversation tonight that I need to go to bed.It's bad enough that I will be falling asleep at work. He assured me that we were not going to be on the phone long. He wanted me to start getting my proper rest however he wanted to let me know he enjoyed spending time with me. I felt the same way we said good night and got off the phone.

Chapter 7

Getting the kids up are always a hassle but still managed to get LaTrice to the salon on time. I went in to speak to Nicole kissed LaTrice and told her I would be back going to drop your sister off at nana's house & call me if you get done before I come back. In my mind, I was thinking I can drop Serenity off and call Abdul to maybe have breakfast or lunch with him. I enjoy his stimulating conversation. Get to nana's house and had to sit down spend some time with her just didn't want to drop off and leave. After spending an hour or so with her I realized I left my phone in the car. Nana I am going to leave now see you tomorrow, kiss Serenity and tell her to be a good big girl. I get to the car I had fourteen missed calls. One from Abdul, three from an unfamiliar number, and ten was from Nicole.

Even though I wanted to call Abdul first I didn't because Nicole is the one that has my child and I need to make sure she is ok knowing LaTrice she is complaining about she is hungry or doesn't like her hair. When I called Nicole, she was crying frantically and screaming. What's wrong Nicole she said I need you to come to Williams Memorial hospital I said why she say LaTrice had been shot. What the fuck do you mean my baby has been shot?! I am racing to the hospital. Nicole gave the stylist Dreana the phone. What happened as I am yelling and crying? Tyrone came in with a gun and told Nicole if he cannot have you can't anybody, he raised his gun and shot twice. LaTrice tried to stand up to run and he shot her. Shot her where? It looks like the head I'm unsure. I started to drive faster than the 90 mph that I was always driving. Where is that son of a bitch now? He ran out she replied. Pulling up at the hospital I parked right in the front while I was running in the attendant told me I could not park there I ignored him and asked at the information desk what room is my daughter is in. She was on her cellphone laughing and talking as if she did not hear me.

I looked at her name tag her name was Ms. Cooper I screamed and looked her in her eyes I am trying to find out what room my daughter is in. She put her call on hold and looked her name up she said that she is currently in surgery on the fourth floor. I tried to wait for the elevator, it was taking too long. I took the steps and ran as fast as I could. On the fourth floor, I went to the desk and asked for the status of my daughter. The nurse pulled her up in the system and stated that she is still in surgery and if I could have a seat that as soon as Dr. Xavier comes out, he will speak with you. Of course, I could not sit I paced back & forward from wall to wall crying & praying. After thirty minutes passed by, I asked for an update. The nurse said hello my name is Kelsey who are you needing me to check on? I couldn't cuss her out because she was too nice, and she acted as if she was genuinely wanting to help me.

Nurse Kelsey said that Dr. Xavier is a great doctor and has been a doctor for over twenty years that your daughter is in great hands, she prayed with me and hugged me and I broke down in her arms. I feel like my heart has been run over by a Mack truck and I can't breathe my kids is all that I have they need me, and I need them. I look up at the tv and see the salon on news talking about the shooting they said the suspect is still on the loose. The news aired the surveillance video on what happened I am hurt and enraged and want him found immediately. The video has a clear angle on what he looks like and praying someone would come forward. Nurse Kelsey watched it with me, and I watched the tears roll down her eyes she had so much compassion she explained to me that her nephew was shot by a stray bullet by a police officer that just got on the force and used his gun carelessly.

She sees so many guns shot victims come in the hospital of all different ages. Dr. Xavier came in looking for the mother of LaTrice I almost tripped over a chair trying to get to Dr. Xavier. How's my baby Dr? LaTrice is currently in ICU she has a bullet womb to her chest. It passed all main arteries, and we were able to move all bullet fragments. She will remain in ICU for the next 24 hours for strict monitoring before being moved to a regular room. In ICU its only 2 visitors of the immediate family can come in at a time. The nurses are getting her comfortable in her room. Once she can have visitors, I will have nurse Kelsey come out to get you. I know it's hard please allow us about an hour. She is very fragile, and we must make sure we handle her with extreme caution. Thank you, Dr. Xavier!!

Chapter 8

Pacing back & forward awaiting to see LaTrice, making my phone calls to check on Serenity and to update Nana on what's going on. My mind was everywhere I didn't think to call anyone. While on the phone with nana Abdul called, I explained to him what was going on where are you he asked? I am at Williams Memorial on the fourth floor I am waiting to see her she will be in ICU for the next 24 hours and they still have not found him. Found who? Tyrone, that is my friend Nicole's ex-boyfriend. I explained to him what was told to me and what I saw on the news. He asked his last name I said Reese he is from the Westside. Abdul said he will be on his way to the hospital I told him he didn't have to come. He said he was and asked did I need anything. Nurse Kelsey came to me and to check on me to make sure I didn't need anything.

She gave me an update that they are getting LaTrice settled in, and it will not be too much longer. No, I don't need anything, and thank you for letting me know. I called Nicole after she visited the hospital, they took her to the police station for questioning and would not let her talk or see anyone. I hope they find Tyrone and put him under the jail unless my crazy cousins get to him first. The news repeating & updating the story shows an actual picture of him other than the surveillance camera footage. It also shows the grey Toyota Tundra with the tag number he was driving. With this information, I pray that he will be found soon. His target was Nicole meaning he may try to come back if he finds out that he did not shoot her.The day is turning in tonight I went to the nurse's station and asked for an update on LaTrice she stated that she will page Dr. Xavier to get the status. I looked to my right I see Abdul walking in with his arms spread wide to hug me I instantly went into his arms and hugged him and started to cry again. He hugged and cried with

me. As we were hugging nurse Kelsey came to let me know I can finally see my child. She explained that when I go in to remain calm that she will have tubes on her & please do not upset her by crying screaming or anything. She is currently in an induced coma, and she can sense and feel. What do you mean coma? The nurse stated the Dr. will explain more. When we get to the room Dr. Xavier was standing outside LaTrice's hospital room reading a chart. He went over that she is in an induced coma for her body is not overwhelmed to heal. It will aid in her healing process and our goal is for her to make a full recovery. Don't be alarmed he stated.

I am finally able to go in and see LaTrice I had to hold back the tears to see her lying in the hospital bed with tubes in her mouth & nose with needles in her arms. I stood over her and prayed. Dear heavenly father, I know anything is possible for those who believe. I believe in you.

I come to you today asking for healing for LaTrice. I ask you to come and take your place in the spirit of the doctors, nurses, and specialists who will aid LaTrice in her medical needs. I believe nothing is impossible in your hands of power, healing, and your heart of love, mercy, and compassion. Please lay your hand on LaTrice and give her a full recovery. I'm also praying for everyone in this hospital in Jesus' name Amen!

I looked over at Abdul and noticed he had something on his shirt and arm. I did not want to mention it while in the room with LaTrice. As the nurse came in, they stated they needed to freshen LaTrice up and change her catheter and asked could we step out. They stated that I could go shower grab something to eat and if I wanted to spend the night, they will set me up a sleeping area near LaTrice room. I will go shower grab clothes and check on my baby girl and will be right back. Abdul stated he will ride with me. I asked was he driving his car or mine he quickly said yours ok cool I didn't think much of it.

When we got in the car, I told him that he had something red on his shirt and arm he looked and said damn! He explained that before he called me, he was painting and drop the paintbrush when I gave him the news. Abdul said before we stopped by your house can you stop by Arthur's department store. I told him sure, but I don't want to be gone long because I needed to get back to the hospital with LaTrice. I stayed in the car to call the hospital just to make sure LaTrice was still fine. They explained that she is still in stable condition, and they will make sure they take great care of her. Abdul got back in the car asked when we got to my apartment can he shower, and I said sure. In Arthur's, he bought a pair of jeans, a shirt, boxers, and socks. We get home I let him shower first because I wanted to go ahead and pack Serenity more clothes as well as pack me an overnight bag with snacks the vending machine at the hospitals are expensive. I was standing in the mirror brushing my hair into a ponytail Abdul came behind me with his towel wrapped around his waist.

He started to massage my shoulder and went on to say how he hate that all of this is happening and that he didn't want me to overexert myself and end up sick or body shutting down for exhaustion. Sit down for a minute and take a deep breath even if it is just for 20 mins then we can leave. Abdul was making sense because I have not had any sleep, I did not eat anything, and I have an excruciating headache. He told me to lay down for a minute I told him I needed to shower. He knows but for now let me give you a quick massage. He massaged my body from head to toe and I must admit it felt so good, but I knew I had to get up. When he got done with my feet massage, I told him I know I am sweaty and let me go ahead and shower while u get dressed. While I was in the shower, I heard the door open and close I didn't think anything about it. I got out of the shower and asked did he go out the door he said yes, he did he threw his clothes away because they had a paint smell and the clothes were old, he didn't want them anymore.

As we prepared to leave, and he assisted me in grabbing the bags & snacks he also grabbed the trash.

While we were grabbing the things, I was thanking him for being a listening ear and being there for me. His pleasure is what he always says. He opened the car door for me on the passenger side and he drove me to nana's house. I didn't want her to meet him because I was still trying to figure him out. Being a school kid is different from being an adult. Pulling up at nana's house she immediately heard me pull up & opened the door and hugged me with several questions back-to-back. I grabbed Serenity and hugged her tightly while tears roll down my eyes. I will be back soon baby going to check on your sister. She was happy to see me and thought I was taking her with me, I can't she started to cry it hurt to leave her, but I had no choice she was too young to be at the hospital. I wouldn't be able to care for her properly there. I will be back as soon as possible baby love you I gave her a kiss and hug and

walked out. Driving to grab a meal at Nichelle's before we head back to the hospital. I know that restaurant will feel me up it's a black-owned soul food restaurant and it is delicious. Abdul started to explain how he cares for me that he has not found anyone that measured up with the chemistry that we share. I somewhat agree but I am not in the mood to be all mushy right now because I am worried about my child. I listened to him as he talked, I didn't have a response. He mentioned that he would do anything for me to make me happy and keep me and my kids away from danger and never hurt again. I was thinking to myself while that was a deep statement but that is something that we can discuss later.

Chapter 9

Arriving at the hospital it seems like it took us forever to get back. I went to the nurse's station to get an update on LaTrice. She is in stable condition nothing has changed normally it doesn't during an induced coma we only monitor, per the nurse that's on duty. I looked at her name tag nurse Patricia it read. She was a nice older lady she said normally we do not allow anyone to spend the night in the ICU with the patient however nurse Kelsey spoke to her before she left and told me to make you feel comfortable. I smiled and said thank you and please tell her to thank you I appreciate the staff at this hospital. Abdul asked did I need anything before he left, and I said no. I told him to call or text me when you make it home. He kissed me on the cheek and kissed LaTrice on the forehead and told her to feel better soon and I gotcha.

Abdul left and I started to set up my sleeping areas with the sheet, covers, and pillows that were provided for me. Before I laid down, I had to hold LaTrice's hand and say a prayer to God for healing once again. The sun is shining through the window. I was up early before the sunrise awaiting Dr. Xavier to make his rounds and get to LaTrice's room. I called to check on

Serenity and to let her hear my voice and to tell her that I love her. I held LaTrice's hand as I cried out a morning prayer for her. Nurse Patricia came in to make sure that I didn't need anything before her shift was over. She assured me that Nurse Kelsey will be coming in and will make sure I am comfortable. Nurse Patricia advised me Dr. Xavier had two patients before LaTrice and will be right in once he is done and breakfast is on the way. I am very pleased with how the staff treats the patients and their families.

Dr. Xavier finally has made it to the room I was so happy to see him. Good morning Ms. Henderson we will be gradually removing your daughter from her

induced coma. Her vital sign has been stable, and she has no swelling. While we take her out of the coma, we will keep her in ICU to monitor her. She will be moved to a regular room if everything goes well tomorrow and from there, we can consider letting her go home. The nurse will be in soon to check her vitals again and to make sure you don't need anything or if you need to go home, we have a nurse on duty that can sit only with your daughter until you come back in four-hour increments. Thank you so much Dr. Xavier I will be here for a few more hours and may leave to check on my youngest daughter. Nurse Kelsey comes in to check on me to make sure I didn't need anything. She said she left me in capable hands with Nurse Patricia. Yes, you did Nurse Kelsey she was a sweetheart. I kissed LaTrice on the cheek and told her I was going to walk around the hospital to stretch my legs and find myself a cup of hot chocolate. Getting on the elevator I shared it with a janitor he introduced himself. Hi, my name is Robert hello Robert I did not want to give him my

name I was not really in the mood to get to know anyone. You look pretty this morning miss lady. Thank you, the elevator, finally opened he came behind me. I didn't think anything about it. I went to the café to get my hot chocolate and he was behind me getting coffee. He gave the cashier money to pay for both of our purchases. Thank you, Robert he said my pleasure. You never gave me your name I didn't give it to you I replied. Robert no disrespect I am just trying to relax alone and get my mind right. I look behind me he is still walking and talking to me. Sir why are you following me and talking to me. He says that he is on break and feels if I let him walk away then he will not see me again and he wants to get to know me. Robert per your name tag don't you work here. I will see you are around, but I am not interested. I have a lot going on if you don't mind have a great day! He specifically told me that he going to have me just watch.

Enough is enough it is time for me to get back to the room. I couldn't even have a piece of mind.

Getting back out of the elevator on the floor that LaTrice is on as I'm walking to her room Abdul called me, he was checking on LaTrice and making sure that I didn't need anything. He could tell by my voice that I was a little uneasy. I begin to tell him about the guy named Robert that works at the hospital he asked a few detailed questions we laughed about it. However, I let him know how he was extremely annoying and somewhat aggressive. Abdul was a great listener and seems to be intrigued by the conversation. I am coming to see you after work and bring you food do you need anything he asked? No food is enough the hospital food does not taste the best and would love to have outside food. I packed enough clothes for tomorrow, and I don't want to leave because they are taking her out of the induced coma, and I want to be here.

Abdul arrived with a plate from the restaurant Regina's the food there is delicious. I looked in the bag and it was steak & potatoes my favorite with a large, sweet tea. He didn't stay long at all he was acting as if he was in a rush. I told him thank you I appreciate you. He leaves I looked at the tv it shows that they found Tyrone dead at a park, and it looks like a homicide and awaiting the autopsy. I called Nicole to check to see if she was still at the police station because she has not called to check on LaTrice or anything. She did not answer my call I'm praying that she is ok, but it is not like her to not reach out to me and especially call to check on her godchild. I called to tell Abdul since he was just leaving to let him know he did not answer the phone. Nana called me to tell me she was looking at the news and saw it and wanted to check on us. I updated her on everything that Dr. Xavier told me. I placed her on speakerphone, and we said a prayer for LaTrice.

It was amazing that slowly but surely how they have medications that can place you into a coma and medications to wake you up from it. It seems that now the doctors can try and play God well that's my opinion. I noticed LaTrice's fingers moved I pressed the button to the nurse's station to let them know. Nurse Kelsey and another nurse per her tag name were Nurse Sutton she was not smiling or anything as if she was in a bad mood, I said hello to her, and she barely spoke back. As always Nurse Kelsey is very nice. She checked LaTrice's vital signs, and she said so far so good everything looks normal with her vital signs. She is gradually waking up. I don't want to leave her side I am so excited to see my child open her eyes and talk to me. I started to rub her hair and sing the song I would sing to her when she was a little girl. Thanks for my child by Cheryl Pepsi Riley. Both of my kids have brought so much joy and I would not change them for the world.

I heard a loud noise in the hallway like a piercing scream that said call 911. I peeped my head

out of the room I did not step out because I did not know what was going on. The hospital security went to her and asked what was wrong? She said she went into the breakroom to get a cup of coffee and it is a man in

64

there that has been beaten to a pulp. Security told the nurse to call to go ahead and call 911 and he will go check everything out. Security check him out another nurse ran back to let the staff know what she saw was a man lying there on consciousness that had two black eyes and a bloody nose. She explained that it looks like he was beaten bad it was blood everywhere, but it seems like he was still alive. The police would need to get a report or check the camera's then they can move him to a room to get checked out.

I heard my phone ring while I was being nosey. Abdul called to check on me to see how we were doing I updated him on LaTrice and her progress and the situation that was going on at the hospital. I could only tell him what I overheard so far. He asked was the guy alive I told him I think so.

I called you earlier to tell you about Tyrone, but you did not answer the phone he saw on the news he stated. Abdul explained that he had to work an overnight shift, and he was about to go to sleep to get some rest before he goes to work and will text me on the way to work to see if I'm up and if not, he will call me when he gets off. Sweet dreams and have a good night at work I will be here all-night waiting on LaTrice to wake up.

Police came to the ICU unit to ask questions regarding the beating in the breakroom. Nurse Kelsey asked did the guy worked here, is he a patient or a visitor? Police stated that he was an employee at this hospital by the name of Robert Robinson. I was thinking to myself I wonder is it the guy that tried to talk to me when I went to the café for hot chocolate? One of the nurses started crying and asked where did they take him? They transported him to the second-floor ma'am however he cannot have any visitors at this time he is being checked out by a doctor. She told him that he is her brother and she need to go be there for him and she walked right past him to go check on

her brother. She looked familiar but she walked by so fast I couldn't get a good look at her. Police stated that the security cameras did not capture anything because the security system has been down since the storm last week and no one reported an issue. As of now, there are no leads on who would possibly want to hurt Mr. Roberson.

Chapter 10

LaTrice is woke thank God she looked over at me I was asleep, and I heard her angelic voice say mama why I am here. I jumped up quickly with tears rolling down my eyes. Hey mama baby an accident occurred, and it landed you in the hospital, but we will get to that later right now I only want you to focus on getting better. I called for the nurse to come in to do vitals and to contact the doctor. She asked about Serenity she is with Nana keeping her company while I am here with you. Mama, I feel pain in my body! The nurse is on the way in here she will give you something to ease your pain. Nurse Sutton comes into the room I dread to see her because she is so dry, doesn't smile, or has any type of emotions. She checked the signs and then said the Dr will be in to examine her. Her? She has a name Nurse Sutton you are not a people person at all, are you? I'm fine she said, and she walked out. As she was

walking out Dr. Xavier was walking; he came in with a pleasant smile.

Dr. Xavier what is wrong with Nurse Sutton it's like she walks around numb I have never seen her smile and she is just so dry. Dr. Xavier apologized that I have to experience her be like that he explained that she use to be so joyful and full of life but less than 6 months ago while she was at work she lost her husband, 3 kids, and her dog to a house fire. She received a phone call while she was at work telling her she needs to come home immediately. Oh my God Dr. Xavier my heart goes out to her I understand now. She is stronger than me I would have ended up in a mental hospital. LaTrice is healing well all her vital signs are normal, by the end of the day she should be able to go to a regular room. We are going to bring her something for pain and I will have a nurse to send for her meal to see if she can keep it down and we can go from there. Thank you so much, Dr. Xavier. I will come back tomorrow to do a final checkup before she is moved once she is moved, she will have another Dr on that floor.

We will have a conversation regarding LaTrice and her recovery plan. When the Dr left, I pulled out my hairbrush and started to brush LaTrice's hair. Nicole had just got done with her hair she flat ironed it. I brushed her pretty hair into a ponytail. I called Nana I know she wants to know what is going on with LaTrice she was so happy to hear her voice and she was able to talk to Serenity. Nurse Sutton came in and gave LaTrice her tray to eat and to take her meds. I look at her differently now even though she doesn't think I know about her tragedy I am not going to tell her that I do. My heart goes out to her.

Well, Nicole is calling me.... Hello Nicole, how are you? She sounded down in which is to be expected with everything going on. She asked how LaTrice doing I gave her an update on everything that have been happening. She said at after she left the hospital to get checked out, she was escorted to the police station they asked her several questions and wanted to know

if he was abusive all this time why she never reported anything? She had to be honest and say she was blinded in love with him and thought one day he would change, and she believed that he would. The salon owner called her due to her personal life it places others in danger, and she no longer can work in the salon she needs to come to pick up her belonging immediately. Wow that is crazy you have been at that salon for five years the owner has no remorse for what happened. Do her out your home when you are up to it or take time to get your mind right. My focus right now is LaTrice and I'm glad that the mother fucker is dead he shot my child, and we don't have to worry about him hurting anyone else. My child took that bullet that was meant for you!

Now that LaTrice is in a regular room I'm looking forward to meeting her new Dr to get the game plan. She is eating well her vital signs have been normal her pain is not as bad, and the meds are working. Abdul walked in the door I wasn't expecting you to visit today nice surprise, how are you?

He had us on his mind and wanted to stop by to see if we need anything and to check on us.

A man walked in behind him this man was tall dark and handsome and you can tell by his shirt and his Dr coat that he works out often the way his pants fit and his dick print oh my my my imagination went wild. It's so many things that I would do to him, and I want him to do to me. I was starring so hard he was trying to introduce himself and I didn't hear anything he said. Abdul looked at me and asked was I ok I told him I was great I just felt a little lightheaded. He passed me a bottle of water that I was drinking earlier he says it may help. I was thinking to myself I know who can help me.   Hello, I am Dr. Richard I am the Dr that does the rounds on this side of this floor. LaTrice answered all the Dr questions and he stated that she should be able to go home tomorrow with restrictions until she heals more. I requested for a sit-in nurse until I leave, I wanted to go home and shower and get LaTrice her clothes to be able to go home in the clothes she had on they had to cut them open.

Once again Abdul said that he would take me, and we can drive his truck. I was tired anyway I accepted that offer. LaTrice I will be back as soon as possible. It's ok mama she said I will be ok I am about to take a nap. The sit-in nurse came in to introduce herself her name was Nurse Shannon hello nurse Shannon please take care of my daughter while I'm gone. I kissed LaTrice and went out the door. When we walked out the door before, we got to the elevator and Abdul said he is going to the restroom he will be right back. As the elevator was about to open, I looked to my left and it is the guy, Robert. He was the victim that got beat up. Even though he is not going to get my number I didn't want it to be him. It seems that he could be a decent guy for someone. He was being released from the hospital. It seems like he was scared to talk to me or look me in my eyes.

The elevator open again I told him to go ahead because I was waiting on someone and he went into the elevator before the door closed, he asked for my number again and I said goodbye Robert take care. Abdul came out of the restroom ready to go I pressed the button on the elevator to take us down to the parking deck. This was my first-time riding in his truck a very nice gray Tundra truck. It felt good sitting up high. His a/c was blowing good, nice music playing listening I started singing along to the song. Abdul was trying to sing with me, but I must admit his voice is way better than mine. I was in a better mood because LaTrice is close to coming home and she is doing so much better. I feel I can breathe again. Lord thank you for covering my baby and continuing to cover her praying for her to have a full recovery. Abdul started to tell me once again that he never had chemistry with a woman like he has with me and wish that I would give in and be in a relationship with him.

I had to reiterate that I am not ready for a relationship right now and I must take things slow. I want to enjoy my kids, get a better paying job, find myself loving myself, date from time to time to see what is out there, and eventually, move out of the apartment and get a house for me and my kids. Abdul stops singing with me in the truck. I guess he was a little salty about my statement. We stopped at a red light and noticed that my cousin Johnny pulled up beside us. I rolled down the window and said what's up fat head. Hey big baby he said how is everything going I heard what happen. I said she is better and should be coming home soon. He said OK let me know if you need me, I will be safe, and the light turned green. Abdul sped off as if he put his feet to the pedal. I looked over at him and ask was he ok he said he was fine I said OK. Well, you were about to give me whiplash the way you pulled off. I started back singing as we turned into my apartment. When we walked in, I asked did he want bottled water.

He said no then says it is very disrespectful to be talking to another man while you are in the car with another man. I don't care who I am in the car with if I see my cousin man or woman I am going to speak! Oh, that's your cousin yes Abdul that is my cousin. This is the main reason why right now I am not ready for anything serious I get tired of my attitude and then deal with someone else's attitude I don't have the time or patience for it. He apologized and said he overreacted that he is so used to females that are so disrespectful and sometimes be disrespectful on purpose just to get an emotion out of him. Yeah, ok well I'm going in her room to change LaTrice sheets and pack her clothes, jump in the shower, then we can leave out. You are more than welcome to watch tv in the living room until I am done.

Getting out of the shower I got overheated from how hot the water was. I wrapped the towel around me and went to the refrigerator to grab a bottle of water to help me cool off. When I turned around Abdul was standing behind me he picked me up and put me on the kitchen counter and started to suck on my breast at first I was trying to resist the temptations because I know that was something I was not ready for he started to go down and lick in between my inner thighs and slowly spread my legs wide and start to suck on my clit and slide his tongue in and out my vagina. The more he was licking the wetter I got the more I was into it was driving me insane. I told him to get up I am about to cum he said he wants me to. Then suddenly it seems like my vagina exploded with sensations and when I thought we were done he slid his penis inside of me and begin to slowly stroke inside me. I did not want this to happen and don't understand why I was not firmer with my no. But it feels so good, and it has been a long time since I had a man to make me feel so good sexually. He gently picked me up from the counter turned me around and bent me over and slid his dick in from the back. I was able to fill every inch of his dick as he went in and out. I hope he knows that we still will not be in a relationship when we are done. That is one thing that I am adamite about. I guess I am thinking too much about him making me feel so good. He said he was about to cum I said so am again. We came at the same time, and it was one of the best feelings I have had in a while. Oh shit!! What are we doing I said we were doing fine right? He said I know that no protection and you did not pull out! It was feeling too good I didn't want to stop that feeling. UGGGHH let me wash up so we can go! I'm sorry but don't regret it. What the hell is that supposed to mean? Whatever happens, will happen it's you that have an issue with a relationship, and know you would have a bigger issue to be pregnant by me. Your right. I value our friendship and what we did cannot happen again!

Chapter 11

Arriving back at the hospital and everything is going well. I stopped to purchase LaTrice a teddy bear, a get well soon card, and a balloon. When I walked in, she had a big smile on her face that gave me so much joy I kissed her on the forehead. Nurse Kelsey was checking her vitals she said everything looks great. Abdul said he is leaving to put his car in the shop, and he will call me tomorrow. He left abruptly I said OK talk to you later. The news came on the tv and was talking about the shooting at the salon. Now they are looking for Tyrone's killer. It was a truck and a car in the area around the time and location he was found dead, and they would like for them to come in for questioning. It is the least of my worries because that bastard shot my baby. In my book, he deserves to die. Tyrone must have enemies for him to be found dead after he shot someone. LaTrice said they are talking about me on the news.

Yes, baby, they are it's by God's grace and mercy you are here. In this room you can have company is there anybody you would like for me to call to come to see you. No ma'am just you and I know my sister cannot come up here and I will see her when I get home. I could not sleep because of the excitement of knowing that my baby could be going home. Good morning, a new nurse came in hello, how are you? What is your name pretty lady she asked LaTrice? The nurse said her name is Elinita and she came to take her blood and then someone will come in to take her for X-rays. After that, we will see if you can walk on your own and you would have to make a bowel movement. If the Dr, says everything looks good, then we can work on having you discharged to go home. LaTrice told her that sounds great!! Mama this hospital food does not taste good. I know baby when you get home, I will cook you your favorite meal or stop to get you your food of choice.

Nurse Elinita took her blood to send it to the lab and called in for someone to get her for an x-ray.

Check this out LaTrice the balling is rolling now let's say a prayer that everything turns out great! LaTrice lead us in prayer she had me crying she has an old soul her prayers be so powerful. I can only imagine how her testimony is going to be when this is all over. Hi, ma'am, my name is Johnny I am the tech that will take her for an x-ray if you turn the tv to channel 83 once we get in the room, I will put the code in for you to observe the x-ray and also a nurse will be assisting me. However, parents are not allowed in. I understand just take care of my baby. LaTrice said I will be fine mama I got this. While she was gone, I called my job to give them an update. I have FMLA that protects me. I was approved for 6 weeks. Those weeks come in handy to get things together, make sure the kids are good and I was thinking about registering back in school. I have been working all these years with no high school diploma.

Even though so far it has not been an issue with me finding employment I want to complete it as my personal goal, and I want to eventually attempt to move up in the company or possibly find myself a better job as a career or start my own business. In my life I am always distracted, I put others before me. It's normal for me I never complain about it because that is the type of person that I am. It's always a man in my life and either something is always happening, and it never works out. It may be God's way of telling me I need to be alone for a while and focus on me, love me and realize my worth, and not be blinded by a man's looks, sex, the conversation of them telling me what they think I want to hear, or what they can do for me. I have been trying extremely hard with Abdul and I already crossed the line and we had sex even though it was good, and I was past due in the sex department, it crossed the line of us just being just friends and what I need right now is a good friend only. I'm not ready to be let down or hurt.

Welcome back LaTrice how are you? I'm good mama with a big smile on her face. I saw you on the tv you did a great job! Tech Johnny said on his way out he will let the nurses know that she is back, and someone will be in with lunch. As the nurses come in to hook her blood pressure monitor the fluids, they are giving her as well as the mild medication that slowly goes in her iv for pain. After you eat lunch young lady, we will give you medicine to help you go to the restroom and we are going to go for a short walk down the hall. I'm ready LaTrice said. Even though LaTrice complained about lunch she must be hungry as soon as the food arrived, she ate all of it. It started to make my stomach growl I didn't eat breakfast. I am stepping out to go get lunch from the cafeteria and I will be right back. When I stepped out, I let the nurses know that I was leaving out. I didn't see Nurse Kelsey it must be her day off. Getting off the elevator on the way to get lunch I heard the police talking to a security guard.

The beating that went on with the guy's name Robert the security guard explained that they originally thought the cameras were offline it had a backup drive and there is a code you must enter to access it. After reviewing it they saw a guy & a woman come in behind Mr. Robinson the lady left out quickly looking back as if she saw something she went away from the elevator. Around eight minutes later we saw the other gentleman leave out but never saw Mr. Robinson leave then shortly after that's when a nurse goes in and notice him. We followed the guy to the parking deck with the different surveillance cameras he got into a gray truck and pulled off. Wow, for someone to beat an employee up at a hospital is childish, and I bet it was and frighten probably something stupid that caused it. As I was standing in line to see what they had on the menu I started to wonder what Robert could have done to someone that would want to come to his job to harm him.

It's a good thing that the cameras had a backup to be able to get to the bottom of what happened to him.

Even if I was not interested in him, he didn't seem like a guy that would get himself in any type of trouble. However, they say you cannot judge a book by its cover. Who knows what this guy is into? The food looks good today, the selection looks better than it did yesterday. I try to eat something that you can't get wrong. I will be safe and get fried chicken mash potatoes and corn. Even though I need to drink more water sweet tea would be my choice of drink. I get back to the floor and I see LaTrice walking with the nurse. She was doing a great job I was so happy to see her walking with a big smile on her face. I went to her room to put my food down to walk beside her back to the room. Uh oh, LaTrice said what's wrong I need to potty that's a good thing let's get you to the restroom. I will be right out here let me know if you need me. While she was in the restroom, I was eating my food the fried chicken was so good, I had chicken grease all around my mouth going down my arm.

I put too much ice in my tea I ran out fast it was good and sweet. The nurse came by to change the sheets.

LaTrice came out of the restroom the nurse had her sit in the chair to sit up versus laying in the bed the whole time she said that she is in mild pain. The nurse said that she would bring her some meds to help her ease the pain. Then she can lay back down to allow the pill to work everything she is feeling is normal from what she has been through. It will get better, and you will soon have no pain at all.

Finally, the next morning, for some reason I slept well looking forward to the Dr coming in to see if LaTrice can go home today. Breakfast is here and it's time for her to eat. The nurse came in advice that once the Doctors are done with their briefing, he will be right in. Looking at the cartoon channel and it is a cartoon called Torie Torie it is hilarious it was beautiful to look over at LaTrice and she is laughing. They gave her a small juice and she wanted more I pressed the button to request more juice and water.

Anything for my baby I kissed her on the forehead. I saw Robert pass by the room I told LaTrice I will be right back.

Hello Robert, I didn't think you were back at work. I'm not I am here to see my sister he said. I didn't think you knew my name how dry you were to me. I apologize that I have been going through a lot and I was also worried about my daughter. How is she? She is better hopefully we can go home today. Here is my business card outside of work I run a recreation center and mentor young boys to be raised into great men. I have my own cleaning business and I have a contract here to clean the hospital but due to the fact random guys come to me to beat me up, I may have to cancel my contract. Random guys? Yes, I had a call out and I was in the break room to clean it and a guy came to me saying leave my woman alone before he slices my throat and I asked who his lady was and he better back up out my face. I got up and walked into the elevator and he followed me he had brace knuckles on.

Oh, wow I am so sorry that happened to you. You may need to stop talking to these women with men. That's the problem he said I am single I have been so focused on my business and my mentorship I have not had time to meet anyone. When the boy's mothers that come to get them, I keep it very professional. Wow, it sounds like you are a good guy. Put my number in your phone once I get through this storm I may focus better and once again I'm sorry. Let me get back in here with my daughter have a good day take care.

Good morning, how you're doing young lady? LaTrice told the doctor that she was doing well and had a little pain now and then. Well, doc what is the verdict? All her test results came back normal. Her womb is healing properly she was able to walk, eat, and have a bowel movement seems like you're ready to be discharged. Please take the time to read the discharge papers. You must take your medicine as directed. You will have to follow up with the Dr that is on your discharge paperwork in two weeks.

Mom when you get home, please schedule the appointment. Yes, Dr. I will thank you so much. The nurse will be in shortly with your papers you can start getting dressed.

Chapter 12

It's great to be home and settled and I have both of my babies with me and still have time off work. My phone rings I noticed that it is Abdul I have not heard from him in a week. Hello, how are you? I'm well long time no hear I told you what we did was going to make our friendship awkward. No, it's not awkward for me I just had things going on he said. He asked how LaTrice was doing I said she is ok healing well. He said he was going out of town and wanted to stop by to see me. I said sure he said he will be over shortly. I was cooking breakfast do you want any he said yes. I went in to check on the kids they are still sleeping I will let them sleep until breakfast is done. I have a taste for pancakes. I will make pancakes, bacon, hash browns, eggs.

I woke up hungry and in a good mood. It's a Saturday mix and they took it back to the old school with an old school DJ. DJ Kizzy Rock knows how to get the party started. He has been on the 1's and 2's since the freaknik days in the '90s. Great clean-up music I probably wouldn't have to wake the kids up my music may do it. Knocking on the door it is Abdul he came in with flowers. He handed them to me and kissed me on the cheek. Ahh, thank you. He said he wanted to give me something to make me smile because he knows how hectic things have been since the shooting. I was blushing because he was right and that was a nice gesture. I am going to put my flowers in a vase you can sit at the table I am about to wake the kids up and I will bring your plate. The kids sat at the table with Abdul he carried a conversation with them. I thought I heard someone blow the horn outside I looked out the window it wasn't anyone it was the song on the radio. I noticed that he was not driving his truck. Abdul where is your truck? I got rid of it and just got a car it had too many repair issues and used a lot of gas.

Oh, ok I thought you loved that truck I enjoyed being comfortable on the passenger seat with the a/c blowing. I turned the music off I wanted to be able to sit at the table to enjoy my meal and watch the kids eat. It is such a blessing to sit at the table with my daughters. The kids ate and wanted to lay back down. I gave LaTrice her medicine and let them go back to their rooms and it gives me time to catch up with Abdul to see why he is going out of town. I turned on the tv to watch the morning news and the weather report. In Georgia the weather changes so much before you leave the house you must make sure you know how hot or cold is it going to be or if it's going to rain. Breaking news came on. The newscaster interviewed an officer named Fred Tilson regarding the shooting I was amazed that they were still talking about it. Officer Fred said there is a new lead it and the incident occurred at Williams Memorial Hospital.

A black male contractor employee was beating in the elevator the surveillance cameras were able to confirm what car the suspect was driving; it fits the description of the vehicle that left the scene regarding the shooting of and suspect / victim that shot an African American girl at a hair salon. They are unsure if it is connected but the owner of this gray Toyota Tundra needs to come in for questioning. My mind is thinking so hard my heart is racing I am asking myself could it be Abdul. But why or is he the type to do anything like that? Maybe he let someone use his car. I am so confused should I even ask him. Have I been this blind or have it been once again under my nose, and I was not trying to face the facts? I act as if I did not pay much attention to the news at this point, I don't know who and what I am working with. Or who is sitting across from me eating breakfast? It could be a big coincidence. I asked him where he was going, he said he will probably go to California or New York are you going alone?

I want you and the girls to travel with me. Would you go? You can leave everything here and start fresh. I started to laugh no Abdul my life is here my job, family, friends and I am not planning on moving from Georgia anytime soon. Especially with a man that I am not in a relationship with. LaTrice also needs to be close to her doctors. Then suddenly it seems as if he flipped out on me. Everything I have done for you, and I ask you and the kids to come with me and you won't! Did for me if you are talking about our times at the parks and the food you purchased for me, I will give you the money back and if you are talking about you eating my pussy and the sex you were satisfied as well. Abdul, I think you should leave I am unsure what is going on, but I have never seen you like this. So now you are trying to kick me out you were just nice to me 20 minutes ago. I am tired of you telling me no! I'm doing everything in my power to make you happy to show you I want to be with you, and it is still a no. I'm jeopardizing my life for you, and this is the thanks I get?

Abdul, I never told you to jeopardize your life for me we haven't even been talking for a long time. I told you from day one that I did not want a relationship. I have other things that I am trying to do with my life, and I am not ready I have been through enough. You told me that you respected my decision, and you were ok with us just being friends.

My phone is constantly ringing it may be an emergency. Hello, who is this? Is this Denise yes, it is? This is Robert hi this is not a good time I will have to call you later. Wait I was calling to give you and heads up that you will be contacted by the police why? The guy that fought me in the elevator was shown on the surveillance camera going into your daughters' room as well as one day showing you getting into his truck. OMG really? I'm so sorry I didn't know anything about this. I know it's not your fault but please be careful. Thank you I will I am going to call you later. I got very worried about having Abdul in my apartment he needs to leave. Since you don't want to go out of town with me, I am leaving without you he said.

I am tired of Georgia, and I am tired of these women here. Abdul, why did you beat Robert up? The same reason why I killed that punk-ass Tyrone to make your ass happy I grasped I knew you were pissed at him for shooting your daughter and didn't know if he was coming back to finish the job. I beat that lame dude because he was trying to take you away from me. Abdul how could you do that to people who are you I never asked you to do that and never would have! You need to leave I don't ever want you to contact me again. Don't text me, call me or come see me, don't even send me a letter. So now what? We are enemies now is what you are telling me? I killed for you and now you are trying to erase me out of your life just like that. Abdul, you need counseling I am not understanding your thought process. What I do know is I don't want you here. Are you going to tell on me? They already know you beat that guy up and it's only a matter of time they will track you for Tyrone's murder.

If you don't leave, I am going to pick up the phone and call the police. I strongly advise you to leave and never look back. Goodbye Abdul!!

Two hours have passed, and I have been sitting in the same spot contemplating thinking of all the clues that were being presented once again I was either blinded by the things I can't see, or I always want to see the good in people. In life, everyone has a dark side some can hide it well and some can't. I hate that Robert was beaten up because he didn't deserve it however my heart does not go out to Tyrone; he was not a good person he shot my child, he used to beat on women, sold drugs to kids, and made them sell drugs for him. I have no tv or phone near me complete silence the kids went back to sleep the door was closed so I assumed they heard us fussing back and forward and closed the door.

My phone is ringing and beeping from text messages, but I have no energy to entertain whoever is on the other side of the phone. I just want to lay down and just cry it is so overwhelming. What am I saying or doing wrong when it comes to men? Why is it my eyes are always covered but wide open?

A knock at the door I don't have time for it. Looking out the peephole it looks like a detective. I opened the door and they asked did I know Abdul I said I know him. They asked was I aware that he is a suspect for a beating and a killing. I have been following it on the news I was not aware that he was a suspect. He came by and said he was going out of town. Did he say where? no sir I just told him goodbye and be careful. I am focused on my kids and right now I am extremely tired. Do you have any more questions? Another detective came in and said they found the suspect. I thought to myself did they find Abdul he didn't leave in time.

I can't hate him because in a twisted way I do think that he cared for me. He just took it to the extreme I want him to seek help, but he would be on the run for the rest of his life. No, ma'am, we have no further questions finally I can lock the door and go lay down to take a nap this day I have had a lot of excitement going on and I just want to process it all. As I was looking for the remote to cut the tv off it was another breaking news that came on tv. The suspect that was wanted for questioning for a beating and murder was found dead with a self-inflicted womb to the head in a vehicle. I was shocked by the news and what I was hearing. I started to cry because even though he took a life I didn't want him to take his own life. Even though I told him goodbye I just felt even though I said it one day I would be able to see him again. Now it is so final he just wanted to love and be loved he just didn't know the right way and I was not ready to be who he wanted me to be to him. As I think of when we were kids, he didn't handle rejection well even as a child.

I will miss our long conversations, the time we spent together, and our sing-along in his truck it hurts.

The tv is off I need to lay in the bed I can't take any more right now. As I go into the bathroom, I look down on side of the toilet I see something gold and shiny I pick it up and it was brass knuckles. It made me flashback on Robert telling me that the guy that was hitting him had brass knuckles on. Even though it was misused at least I have a piece of him. I grabbed my phone to take to the bedroom with me. I started to check my missed calls and messages. Abdul called me three times and sent me a text message oh no I could have possibly stopped him from killing himself. Now it is too late. His text message says "I figured that you would not answer the phone for me, and I hope that you would at least read this message. I want to apologize to you. You were honest with me from the beginning but the genuine person that you are I wanted you to myself to protect and love you and the kids forever.

I know you may think that I am a horrible person, but I am not I would have never hurt you or your kids. I wanted you and the girls to be my family I don't have a family my parents are dead with no siblings and the only woman I ever loved died of cancer and I vowed to myself to try and protect the next woman I begin to love at all costs and that was you. You may didn't feel the same about me but you brought me so much joy and I didn't want to lose you. By the time you are reading this text, I probably had the nerve to end my life. There is nothing else left on this earth for me. I feel like I can't find where I fit. Tell the guy that I beat up I apologize I am very territorial and was afraid that he would have you the way I wanted you. I left you a voice mail so you can always remember what I sound like, and I sent you the selfie we took at the park I also recorded us singing in the car I sent that to you by your email. If people say something bad about me, can you, please at least tell them I wasn't a bad person.

I just love hard by any means necessary. My bullet awaits me I love you goodbye!"

I cried myself to sleep woke up with a major headache. LaTrice took care of Serenity for me last night and didn't even wake me. I thought I would get up this morning and it was all a nightmare, but it wasn't I fell asleep with the brass knuckles on my bed. I have been trying to reach out to Nicole she is not answering, and her salon family has not seen her. I turned on the tv they were talking about the body being identified and all the evidence points to Abdul for the shooting and the beating. The only next of kin was an uncle named Antonio Davis he is incarcerated and will be getting out in a few months. A letter was found in his bag he was writing his uncle talking about the new lady in his life that he had been writing him about and how he wanted to change his ways and was tired of being labeled as being aggressive and loving people too hard.

They will be investigating who he was visiting at Williams hospital as well as who the new lady he referenced in his letter is. If they come to my door, I will not be answering this is too much for me. I don't want to be intertwined in all this chaos. How did I get myself into this? I was so sure to be careful to let anyone that enters my life know that I am not ready for anything serious. I need to work on myself. It's time to take the blindfold off use my third eye and start accepting things at face value and see the warning signs and the red flags even in just a friendship. When will I have the man that God designed for me? Or that genuine friendship with no expectations? I feel everyone has a label even if you try to remove it you can never remove the original label. Your label will always be a part of you. (Your past) Sometimes you don't realize a person's original label because you are too busy wanting them to be how **YOU** want them to be. When you finally realize it's too late you have already become blinded by your labels you placed upon them.

Now you are hurt but when you think about it you hurt you. Take off the blindfold! Everyone that enters into your life is not good for you sometimes it may not take long to realize it and sometimes it may take a little longer.

Don't ignore!

The things you don't want to see...

Hello! Collect call from Antonio do you accept? Yes, who is this? Is this Denise? This is Tony what's up bitch you're the reason why my nephew is dead I will be seeing you in a couple of months ...

I wonder what will happen when Uncle Tony get out? Where is Nicole? Will LaTrice be ok after her surgery? What label do Robert have? Is Seneca getting out of jail? Is Nana in danger? Was the missing girl ever found? Is Reginald safe in jail even though he is a preacher now? What labels does Denise have? Your questions will be answered in the next book and more stay tuned...

Thank you for purchasing my first book. I hope you enjoyed reading it just as much as I enjoyed writing it. Follow me on social media on the release dates of my upcoming books.

Please email me your reviews:

AuthorLaTarchaJackson@gmail.com

Follow Author LaTarcha Jackson

Facebook: Labeled

Instagram: Book_Labeled

TO BE CONTINUED.........

The Lotus flower is regarded in many different cultures, especially in eastern religions, as a symbol of purity, enlighten, self-regeneration and rebirth. Its characteristic is a perfect analogy for the human condition: even when its roots are in the dirtiest waters, it rises above the surface to bloom. The Lotus produces the most beautiful flower.

<u>Dedication</u>

I dedicate my book to my daughters Le'Asha & Shandricka. (Pray your sister Fredrica in heaven proud of me to) If no one else knows you young ladies know how much completing this book meant to me. Our middle of the night conversations and scenarios we did it!! On to the next one…

This book is also dedicated to my loved ones that has passed away. To be absent from the body, is to be present with the Lord You are truly missed.

(N.O.H 4 life)

Printed in the United States of America

First Edition, 2020

ISBN   978-0-578-71978-8

AuthorLaTarchaJackson@gmail.com